Zoooo...
Living Poems for Children

Hugh David Loxdale

With original line drawings
by Rita Mühlbauer

Brambleby Books

Zoooo... Living Poems for Children

Copyright© Hugh David Loxdale 2012

Hugh Loxdale has asserted his right
under the Copyright, Designs and Patents Act 1988
to be identified as the Author of this Work.

All Rights Reserved

No part of this book may be reproduced in any form
by photocopying or by any electronic or mechanical means,
including information, storage or retrieval systems,
without permission in writing from both the copyright
owner and the publisher of this book.

ISBN 9781908241139

First published in 2012 by
BRAMBLEBY BOOKS

www.bramblebybooks.co.uk

Cover design and layout by Tanya Warren – Creatix
Cover watercolour by Rita Mühlbauer

Printed on FSC paper and bound by GraphyCems, Spain

Zoooo...
Living Poems for Children

By the same author:

Fascinating Felines (2002)
ISBN 9780954334703, Brambleby Books

The Eternal Quest: A celebration of nature in poetry (2003)
ISBN 9780954334710, Brambleby Books

Blue Skies in Tuscany (2003)
ISBN 9780954334727, Brambleby Books

Bird Words: Poetic images of wild birds (2003)
ISBN 9780954334734, Brambleby Books

The Jena Poems (2010)
ISBN 9780955392894, Brambleby Books

Love and the Sea (2010)
ISBN 9780955392887, Brambleby Books

Nevisian Days: Poetry from a Caribbean Isle (2011)
ISBN 9781908241009, Brambleby Books

Bird of Paradise: Selected Poetry 1968-2011 (2011)
ISBN 9781908241016, Brambleby Books

Dedicated to Winnie and Mary,
keen observers of the natural world

Preface

These poems for children were mostly written whilst my wife Nicola and I stayed in a small wooden summerhouse in Utting in Bavaria, Germany, during the summers of 2004 and 2011. *The Elephant* and *The Giraffe* were written much earlier in Batford, near Harpenden, Hertfordshire, U.K. in 1996 and 1997, respectively, whilst the Limerick *Weed Fancier* was composed in Manchester, U.K. in July 2011. The earlier collection, comprising 18 poems, was lost during several house moves, but was rediscovered during a further move in May 2011, whereafter I completed another 15 poems. The initial idea was to write poetry that children would enjoy, accompanied by suitably pleasing drawings. Also ones that would make children think about the true 'nature of nature', including the environment we live in and conservation of the many species that inhabit the planet with us. Hence, not a sanitized version of life where all the living organisms live happily together without interaction.

Hugh D. Loxdale, Utting, 7th October 2012

Contents

The Elephant	11
The Bactrian Camel	13
Chimps and Bananas	15
Brown Ringlets	17
Camberwell Beauty	19
Cuckoos Will – You Know	21
Bishoo	23
A Sea Lion	25
A Blackbird's Feast	27
After Dark	29
Chips	31
Freckled Girl	33
Hiding the Rhinoceros	35
Lazy as a Daisy	37
Retiring Llamas	39
Tiger	41

The Man and the Bear	43
The Lion's Dinner	45
The Warbler	47
The Warty Newt	49
Up and Down Birds	51
What do you get?	53
Zebras Crossing	55
The Goldfish	57
The Fly and the Kangaroo	59
The Guinea Pig's Lot	61
Weed Fancier	63
The Leopard Slug	65
The Happy Hippo	67
The Adder	69
The Aardvark	71
Selfish as a Shellfish	73
The Giraffe	75

The Elephant

The Elephant is a mighty beast,
It stands three metres high,
And if it stands upon your toes,
It's bound to make you cry.

The Bactrian Camel

The Bactrian Camel has two humps,
One fore, one aft,
A daft arrangement you might think,
But most agreeable
When you are sitting comfortably
In-between.

Chimps and Bananas

Emily likes bananas,
Like the Chimps at the Zoo,
Who eat them aplenty
When there's not much else to do.

They also like apples,
Which they have not yet learnt to peel,
But chew them anyway
With a happy kind of zeal.

Brown Ringlets *

It's a good year for brown Ringlets;
We see them every day.

Flying low amongst the glistening grasses
When the Sun is shining there.

*Butterfly - *Aphantopus hyperantus*

Camberwell Beauty *

The Camberwell Beauty,
We saw it for but a trice,
A dark, black shape
That glided near to us
As we sat and had our tea...
And was gone.

A rare, magnificent sight
To behold;
A lovely butterfly,
So very nice.

*Butterfly - *Nymphalis antiopa*

Cuckoos Will – You Know

The Cuckoo calls by both day and night,
Being very shy it keeps well out of sight.
As such, it is rarely seen,
Small birds hardly know it's been and gone,
Hushed such that it's laid an egg
In their own nest;
It does so sneakily
By right.

Yet it is not very kind for sure
Making poor little Robins, Dunnocks
And warblers do its work,
Rearing a huge, great chick,
Big, as thick as a brick...
And ugly too.

But that's nature, ever knowing.
Meanwhile, the chick keeps growing
Until that day, later in the spring,
When it flies back south...
To Africa,
Very much plumper...

But it does not thank its
Mum and Dad...if indeed,
They are.

Bishoo

There was a black dog called Bishoo
Whose pedigree was never at issue,
Though when he grew old
He alas caught a cold,
And instead of 'woof', barked 'atishoo'.

A Sea Lion

A Sea lion,
Sitting on a rock by the sea,
Got too hot in the spring sunshine
And, in order to cool off,
Stuck his hands in the water.

"Wow! It's a bit nippers
Around the flippers,"
He uttered in his gruff way.

But his friend nearby
On the same rock
Who overheard
Stated intently:
"Don't be a wimp!
You can always clap your hands together
If you need to keep warm."

And so once in the water,
He did and was swiftly
Applauded by the other sea lions
As being very intelligent...

Yet never gave due credit
To his friend for the original
Suggestion.

The moral of the story:
Not all applause is meaningful...
Or merited.

A Blackbird's Feast

A Blackbird one day spied a worm
Which he saw wriggling in the grass.

"Why," he asked, "is the worm
Disporting itself in the Sun?"

"Why," asked the worm, "is that bird
Watching me with evil intent?"

Now though, the bird and the worm
Are united as one.

After Dark

After dark,
The neighbour's cat,
White with grey patches,
Sits under the plum tree;
Its eyes shine like stars.

But unlike Orion's belt,
Only two, not three,
Are ever alight.

Chips

Chips are great to eat,
Chips are fun.
They tend to help you grow...
Until you weigh...like a hippo,
Something like a ton!

Freckled Girl

There was a young girl from Eccles
Who was covered from head to toe in freckles.
One day in the Sun
She counted every one,
But preferred to call them her speckles
(like the hen).

Hiding the Rhinoceros

Where do you hide a rhinoceros,
A strange choice of pet,
If you decide to keep it indoors,
When outdoors it is cold and wet?

A matchbox is not suitable,
Nor is the leaf of a fig,
For unlike a ladybird,
It is surely much too BIG!

Lazy as a Daisy

To sit in a field
Is a perfect way to become lazy...

And watch butterflies pass
Amidst the tall grass,
As the day becomes hot...
And hazy.

Retiring Llamas

It is said that Llamas
Are never known to wear pyjamas.
Instead, they have wool,
Awake and abed,
On their backs, legs and their head.

A most suitable attire
When they are about to retire
To the High Andes...
But not the warm Bahamas.

Tiger

The Tiger,
Silent as a wraith,
Merges into the shadows
Of the jungle.

Is he there – or isn't he?

Maybe it's just the movement
Of a bird rustling the dry leaves…
Or perhaps the wind itself.

Who knows?…

Except the Peacock,
On a branch high up,
Who alone sees those wide paws
And sinuous body below the scrub;
Rust red and white,
The huge head with golden,
Piercing eyes
Ablaze…

And a long swishing tail,
Periodically scaring the flies
That impudently try
And settle on its flanks.

The King – magnificent – rests now.
But soon, as the Sun rapidly sinks
below the western horizon
And the tree frogs begin to croak,
He will be on the prowl,
Looking for a young, tender
Morsel – or two –
On which to feed.

The Man and the Bear

There was a young man from Westphalia
Whose plan was to visit Australia.
But on the way there
He was chased by a bear,
So that his hopes ended in failure.

The Lion's Dinner

One day,
Whilst going for a walk in the savannah,
A Lion met a Gazelle.

Said the Lion to the Gazelle:
"You look like a fine bit of dinner to me!"

"Not so," said the Gazelle,
Who had different ideas.

Suddenly and unexpectedly
Before it could spring,
The Lion was momentarily dazzled
By the bright reflection
Of the Sun shining in its eyes...
Whereupon the Gazelle was gone into the tall
Grass – and safety –
Like a shot.

"That's not fair," murmured the Lion
As it went away hungry.
"That's not playing by the rules."

The Gazelle, not being that far away,
Overheard this and replied:
"What are the rules? They are your rules..."
And then carried on running into the distance...
Obeying the full law of the Gazelle – to survive.

"On reflection," said the Lion,
"I suspect you are right.
That is why I still need to catch you...
And eat it all up."

The Warbler

The Warbler warbles
All summer long,
All June and July in wonderful song,
Before it returns to Africa
Its home, once more,
On one great melodic trip, for sure.

The Warty Newt *

The Warty Newt is not that cute.
Rather it is wet and slimy,
But also very smart in its
Black and orange suit.

It lives in still water, often a pond,
Where it hangs about;
The females laying lots of little eggs
Each wrapped in a water plant frond.

These hatch to become *efts*
That wriggle and squirm a lot,
Eventually to become small newts too
That then leave their watery plot.

They feed on small insects and other tasty fry,
And chew them with much haste,
Though never show the slightest remorse,
And really enjoy the taste.

(Yum, yum!)

Triturus cristatus

Up and Down Birds
(Treecreeper* and Nuthatch+)

On our plum tree,
Old and tall,
The Treecreeper,
She of white breast
And sharp claw,
Climbs up till on high,
Only then to fall,
To fly down
And start the process
Once more.

The Nuthatch though
Is cleverer still:
She climbs both up and down...
In little runs...
To grab a nut
On the bird table
And then despatch it
With her hard, sharp bill,
Whilst holding it firmly
In a crevice in the bark.

Light orange and grey,
With a black eye stripe and loud call,
The Nuthatch is a fine bird
But no songster,
Certainly not a lark...
At all.

Certhia familiaris; + Sitta europaea

What Do You Get?

What do you get if you cross
A Llama with a Giraffe?

Answer: A laugh!

What do you get if you cross
A Llama with a Whale?

Answer: A very strange animal indeed.

Zebras Crossing

Zebras are very stripy
And have difficulty crossing the road,
Especially when there's lots of traffic –
Like speeding lorries with a heavy load.

Whilst crossing rivers is more dangerous still,
As the Crocs await them there,
To eat their fill of Zebra steak,
Without tears, without a care.

The Goldfish

The Goldfish is a cold fish,
Swimming in its pond,
Till the Sun arises
And warms it up,
And allows its tail
To splish...and splash.

The Fly and the Kangaroo

Why the Kangaroo hops so high
Was once considered by a fly,
As it landed one day for a ride
On its tail, the toughest old hide,
And was henceforth immediately,
And unceremoniously,
Flicked back into the sky.

The Guinea Pig's Lot

Guinea Pigs are funny beasts;
They tend to squeak a lot.
Here we keep them as cuddly pets,
But in Peru, they go into the Pot.

Weed Fancier

There was a slim woman from Leeds
Who had a mad passion for weeds,
She watered and sowed them,
Trimmed and hoed them,
And was renowned for her kindness and deeds.

The Leopard Slug *

The Leopard Slug is very handsome,
Covered in smart black patches,
Yet, as every lettuce knows,
He very soon despatches.

So be wary of his stealth and cunning,
Especially if your beans are running,
Since he climbs up as well as prowls,
Though unlike the real leopard,
Seldom, if ever, growls.

*Limax maximus

The Happy Hippo

When is a Hippo happy?
This is a good question to ask;
They certainly like floating in water,
Or on sandbanks where they bask.

They also come on land at night
To graze the fresh green grass,
Yet rarely stay too long,
When the lions have finished their fast.

Perhaps they just like being lazy.
Lying around most of the time,
A habit they recommend
And to them, they find sublime.

The Adder *

Is the Adder a subtractor?
It is if it bites your nose...
So be careful when you lie in the grass,
And also safeguard your toes.

*Vipera berus

The Aardvark*

The Aardvark, ever bold,
Never makes hard work
Of making a hole;
On the contrary, like the Mole,
It's very adept,
And just keeps digging downwards,
As if for gold.

*Orycteropus afer

Selfish as a Shellfish

Shellfish can be very selfish,
Remaining clammed up
For hours,
And rarely communicating with their fellows,
Except when feeding,
And also when the call of love
Loosens their grip.
Then they open their shells a bit wider
Than usual,
To take a peek outside,
To see who's around
And maybe say their hellos.

The Giraffe

When a Giraffe
Has a laugh,
It can rarely be heard,
Except by a bird,
High in the sky!

About the author

Hugh David Loxdale was born in Horley, Surrey, England and is of English, Welsh and Irish descent. He has been interested in natural history since the age of five and is an entomologist by profession. He started writing poetry when he was seventeen. This is the author's ninth book of poetry. He is married and presently lives in Utting and Augsburg, Germany.

About the Illustrator

Rita Mühlbauer is a freelance artist and illustrator living in Munich. She has drawn as long as she can remember, initially, as she says, angels, animals, plants and portraits of people. Later she started to paint. After a busy period of study at the Academy of Fine Arts in Munich, these themes came back to the forefront of her imagination, however sometimes in a new (for her) surrealistic context.

The present line drawings are the result of both her intensive studies of nature in its various rich forms and guises over many years, as well as being inspired by reading these poems for children.

Other natural history books by Brambleby Books

ISBN 9780954334772

Feathers and Eggshells – A bird journal of a young London girl
Natalie Lawrence
A delightful journal by a young London girl, describing the wild birds of Hampstead Heath using drawings, photographs, prose and poetry.

ISBN 9780955392832

Garden Photo Shoot – A Photographer's Year-book of Garden Wildlife
John Thurlbourn
A charming illustrated garden wildlife book.

ISBN 9780955392818

What's in your Garden – A book for young explorers
Colin Spedding
This book, for children aged 7-11, is all about exploring and discovering nature.

ISBN 9781908241078

Buzzing!
Anneliese Emmans Dean
A potpourri of fun poems about small garden creatures, accompanied by their colour portraits.

www.bramblebybooks.co.uk